Wasted

by

L. A. Weatherly

For every Luke and Gemma

First published in 2012 in Great Britain by
Barrington Stoke Ltd
18 Walker Street, Edinburgh, EH3 7LP

www.barringtonstoke.co.uk

ISBN: 978-1-84299-818-2

Printed in China by Leo

1

A Leap of Faith

Toby Cutler lay flat on the deck of a rotting Thames cargo boat. The man he knew as Black Bob looked up from the tiller and glared into the wet night.

"I knowsh you're about, young varmint," snarled Black Bob. His voice

was harsh and slurred from the rum he had been drinking all evening. "And when I find ye, I'll give 'ee summat to think on." He smashed his fist on the boat's planking.

There was a sound of splintering wood. From his hiding place behind a pile of greasy rope, Toby could see Bob's shadow in the moonlight. He saw the head tip back and the outline of a bottle upturned against the yellow glow of the riverside gas lamps.

Black Bob coughed and wiped his sleeve across his mouth. Then he slumped against the tiller and almost asleep, he steered the

boat upriver on the evening tide.

Toby shivered in the bitter wind and thin icy drizzle. For two years this stinking boat had been his prison. Now he had finally worked out how he could escape. It was risky. But it was a risk he had to take.

Somewhere on the other side of the river, a clock chimed nine times. Toby pulled his ragged jacket up around his neck and waited.

It was Saturday night. Every Saturday

Black Bob went on shore and sold
whatever he had been able to steal from
the cargoes he had carried all week. With
the money, he bought rum – fiery, black
rum that came from the navy ships docked
further down the Thames. Then he tied up
to his mooring, chained Toby to the cross-
planks and drank every last drop.

Toby closed his eyes and thought of
how he had lived for the last two years.
Every day, in between deliveries, Black
Bob tied a rope around Toby's middle and
pushed him over the side to look for scrap

metal in the stinking Thames mud. If he found something, he was fed. If he didn't, he went hungry.

Toby clenched his teeth. It was all his Uncle Michael's doing. Two years ago he had appeared at Toby's cottage. He had good news, he claimed. He knew of a cabinet maker in London who wanted an apprentice. Uncle Michael asked if Toby would accept the job.

A lump rose in Toby's throat as he remembered his mother's joy.

"It's a chance to make a new life, son," she had whispered even though there

were tears in her eyes. "You go. We'll look out for ourselves."

Toby remembered his own square-shouldered promise. "I'll send a sixpence home, ma. You wait and see." Because, as an apprentice, he'd soon be earning a bit of money.

The lump grew in Toby's throat but he didn't cry. He had stopped crying the moment after Michael had dumped him on Black Bob's cargo boat and sold him for exactly a sixpence.

Toby crept out from behind the rope and crawled over to the shore side of the

boat. Over the slap and trickle of the water against the hull, he could hear Black Bob snoring.

Across the river, ten chimes rang out. Toby felt his stomach tighten with nerves. Any minute now, Oyster Jim's barge would pass within a couple feet of them.

Oyster Jim carried a small sail which took him up river faster than Black Bob's cargo boat. But even more important, he moored a good mile away.

Every Saturday, Toby had watched Oyster Jim slide past them after the ten bells rang out. And little by little a plan had taken hold in his mind.

As the two boats passed near each other, he would jump onto Jim's barge and hide. When the barge slowed down to tie up, somehow he would scramble on shore.

Toby felt fear lurch in his guts. He knew that if he fell into the water he would drown. Worse, he knew that if Black Bob tracked him down, his life would not be worth living.

The moon slid from behind the clouds. At the tiller, Black Bob was still snoring. The tide under his feet told him all he needed to know to steer the boat.

Toby slithered silently over the edge of the boat. Then he held onto a rusty iron ring and braced his feet against the hull.

Slowly the flickering lantern that hung from the prow of Oyster Jim's barge drew closer to Black Bob's boat.

Toby waited until the two boats were

almost touching. Then, saying the only prayer he knew – *God Help Me* – he jumped across the oily water.

Thump! Toby landed heavily beside a pile of dirty rags. As fast as he could he scrambled underneath them and curled up like a hedgehog.

Even though Oyster Jim hated Black

Bob, Toby knew he would hand him back if there was a penny to be made.

"Wozzat?" growled a drunken voice.

A greasy head appeared through a hatch.

Toby held his breath. The head was

just in front of him. A sharp beaky face looked around.

"Nuffink," muttered Oyster Jim. "Pour us another noggin, you daft lump."

The head disappeared and the hatch slammed shut.

In the darkness Toby let out his breath. For the first time he was grateful that almost every man on the river drank themselves stupid most nights.

Half an hour later, Toby crawled from

under the pile of rags over the side of
Oyster Jim's barge, and got ready to jump
again. In front of him a line of rickety
wooden poles grew out of the oily black
water. Rough planks nailed across them
formed a kind of ladder up onto the bank.

Toby muttered his prayer, grabbed hold of a wooden plank and hung on for dear life.

"You didn't ought to be there," said a raspy voice above him.

Toby's stomach went cold.

Tears welled up in his eyes. It was
all over.

"Heh," said the voice. "Gimme
your hand. It's dangerous round 'ere. I'll
help you."

2

A New Friend

"Well I never!" The raspy voice had
turned into a boy the same age as Toby.
He had a bright cunning look to his face
and a wide friendly grin. "You look like
a mud puppy!"

Toby was so relieved that he hadn't

been grabbed by the throat and dragged
back down the river, he couldn't speak.

"Jack Riley's my name," said the boy.
"There ain't nothing I don't know around
here." He grinned again. "'Cept you
of course."

Toby straightened up and introduced
himself to Jack.

"Mmm," said Jack when Toby had

finished the story of his life in two minutes.

"When was the last time you ate, then?"

"Two days ago," said Toby. As he
spoke he suddenly felt horribly weak
and hungry.

"That's disgustin', that is," said Jack.
He put his hand on Toby's shoulder.

"You follow me, young Toby." He
laughed and held his fingers to his nose.

"But not too close, mind. Not till we
get you a new suit of clothes."

Toby stared at him.

"But how can we do that? It's late and I haven't a farthing."

Jack laughed. "Time don't matter and no-one has any money." He held up a stubby finger as if
he was testing the wind. "Good drying weather, though, now the rain has

stopped. Come on."

Toby followed Jack down a narrow cobbled alley, across a muddy street and into a crumbling stone courtyard.

By now a good breeze was blowing and sure enough damp clothes were

hanging out of the windows to dry.

Toby watched in amazement as Jack shinnied up the side of the houses and

one by one snatched a pair of trousers, a shirt, and a jacket. He was just about to grab a thick blanket when a woman's face appeared at the window.

"Thief!" she bawled at the top of her

voice. "Stop, thief!" There was a sound of doors slamming.

Jack landed like a cat and zig-zagged back down the alley.

Toby ran after him, trying as hard as he could to stop his muddy feet from slipping on the cobblestones.

Ten minutes later, Jack and Toby ducked through a broken wooden gate and threw themselves on the ground. As they

waited in the darkness, Toby pulled off
his rags and began to rub at the mud
that covered his arms and legs. It was a
hopeless job.

"Hold on," said Jack. He pointed
across the yard. "I think I see just what
you need."

In a corner half hidden by shadow was
a large wooden rain barrel. Jack got up
and put his hand inside it.

"How about a wash
before dinner?"

Toby peered through the tavern
window. Inside it was crowded and noisy
and full of smoke. But at least it was warm.

"How will we get food in here?"
he asked

Beside him, Jack cocked his head.
"Fancy your chances begging?"

The thought of squeezing through a
roomful of drunks, begging for money
made Toby feel sick. But he was so

hungry, he felt sick anyway.

"Thing about drunks," said Jack as they pushed through the doorway and found a place in the corner, "is they're either mean or soppy."

"What do you mean, soppy?" said Toby. All the drunks he had ever known were either mean, very mean or violent and mean.

"Slobbering on about how things were better when they was younger," muttered Jack. "You know. All soft in the head."

He pointed. "Look at that one."

Toby looked. A red-nosed man in a worn jacket sat on a bench with his back to the wall. In front of him was an almost empty bottle.

Every few minutes a huge sigh passed through the man's large body and he slumped lower against the wall. Finally he bowed his head and wiped his nose with his sleeve.

"What did I tell you!" said Jack triumphantly. "Soppy as they come."

He gave Toby a shove. "Go on. Get a farthing out of him before he drinks it."

Toby bit his lip. "What should I say," he whispered.

Jack rolled his eyes. "How about 'Got a farthing for a hungry lad, guv'nor?'"

Toby got up and dodged around swaying bodies.

"Excuse me, guv'nor," he whispered to the red-faced man. "Can you spare a farthing for a hungry boy?"

The man looked up. He reached into his pocket and pulled the linings inside out. Nothing.

"'Ave a drink, instead," he muttered and held up the almost empty bottle.

At that moment there was a crash of broken glass and everyone went quiet.

In the middle of the

room a short, tubby man with round gold glasses and a moustache was standing in front of a huge black-bearded sailor.

The tubby man was waving a black book.

The sailor was waving a broken chair.

"My name is Thomas Barnardo," cried the little man. "I have come to spread the word of the Lord." He held up the book in his hand. "Listen to the Lord's message. His kindness is your salvation."

"Chuck 'im out!" cackled a woman in a torn scarlet dress.

"We don't want none of your palaver 'ere," yelled a grimy weaselly-looking man. "Toss your book on the fire."

A loud guffaw went round the room.

To Toby's astonishment the little man climbed onto a table and shouted louder. "Be kind to your neighbour and the Lord will be kind to you."

"So what?" bellowed the huge sailor and with one meaty hand, he picked up the little man and lifted him off the floor.

Another chair went over and more bottles smashed.

Suddenly Toby found himself staring into the eyes of the

little man with the gold glasses. They were blazing. But not with anger, Toby realized with a jolt. It was something else.

A hand grabbed his collar. "Let's get out of 'ere," shouted Jack. "The constables are coming!"

Toby and Jack lowered their heads and shoved through the broken tables and wrestling bodies. A minute later, they were in the street.

The sound of whistles grew louder.

"You there! Stop!"

For the second time that night, Jack and Toby ran for their lives.

3

A Light in the Darkness

It was Toby who saw her first.

He and Jack were hiding in a stable
yard when they heard the creak of wooden
wheels. Toby put his head over the wall.
An old woman was pushing a cart piled
with baked potatoes.

"Let's ask if she's got any broken ones," whispered Toby.

"Don't be daft," said Jack. "You  pretend you're sick and while she's not looking, I'll grab two big ones."

Toby swallowed. "What if someone sees ...?"

"They won't," said Jack.

With a pounding heart, Toby clutched his stomach and stumbled down the street.

"Ma'am! Ma'am!"

The old lady stopped her cart. In the murky street light, her round face was as

wrinkled as an oak apple. She smiled at
the two boys.

"You young 'uns look starved!" she
said kindly. "Take these!"

Then to Jack and Toby's amazement,
she handed them each a big potato and
set off down the cobbled street.

Neither Toby and Jack moved. It was

almost as if they had forgotten that
kindness existed anywhere.

"Let's go back to the stables,"

whispered Toby. Somehow the potato was too precious to eat in the street.

A wide grin spread across Jack's face. "Just what I was thinking, mate."

The stables were warm and steamy from the two horses tethered inside.

Toby and Jack kicked some straw into a corner and made themselves a bed. Then they ate half a potato each and fell into a deep sleep.

★ ★ ★

Toby awoke with a jerk.

A lantern was swinging above his head.
In the bright circle of light, Toby saw the
dark shapes of two men. He felt in the
straw beside him. Jack was gone.

Toby's mind exploded with terror.

"Don't kill me," he screamed. He felt
for the potato in his pockets. "Take this.
It's all I have."

One of the men bent down and laid his

hand on Toby's shoulder.

"We don't want your food, lad," he said. "We are here in the Lord's name. We want to help you."

Toby stared into the man's face. He had a moustache and wore round gold glasses. For a split second he wondered if he was dreaming. "You're the man I saw in the tavern," he gasped.

The little man looked grave and turned to his companion.

"It is a terrible thing that a lad so young should be in such an evil place, Mr. Williams," he said. "Now do you see why my work is so important?"

"Indeed, I do,"

replied the man holding the lantern. "Come lad, we will give you food and a roof over your head."

Toby didn't move. He stared into the tubby man's face.

"How do I know you aren't lying? How do I know you won't sell me back to Black Bob?"

The little man held Toby's thin dirty hand.

"My name is Thomas Barnardo. I have a house for homeless children." He spoke gently. "I come in kindness. Let me help you."

Kindness. Toby's bottom lip began to

tremble. Suddenly, the terrible despair of the last two years welled up like a fountain inside him.

He crumpled into a heap and sobbed his heart out.

Up in the rafters Jack Riley clenched his teeth and didn't move. There was no way a grown-up was taking him off. Jack

didn't trust grown ups. He'd heard too many of their lies.

Below the two men helped Toby to his feet.

"I need Jack," cried Toby in a choked voice. "He's my friend."

Up in the darkness, a prickling feeling crawled over Jack's body. No-one had ever said they needed him. Jack bit his lip. Maybe they would never say it again.

As George Williams pulled open the stable door, Jack knew he didn't want to be on his own anymore. He needed Toby as much as Toby needed him.

He let go of the rafter and dropped onto the straw.

"Well done, lad," said

Thomas Barnardo as if he was used to boys dropping out of nowhere. He put his hand on Jack's shoulder.

"Hot cocoa all round tonight, don't you think, Mr. Williams?"

George Williams pulled the stable door shut behind them.

"Capital idea, Dr. Barnardo," he replied.

4

Two Helping Hands

Thomas Barnardo stood in front of the
house that was his home for children and
said a small prayer to himself. Through
the window, he could see Jack Riley and
Toby Cutler hammering soles onto a big
pile of old boots.

"Those two lads are doing well," he murmured to George Williams, standing beside him.

"They're good boys," agreed George Williams. "The others like 'em, too."

Thomas Barnardo looked over his glasses. "I've noticed that too," he said slowly. "It's given me an idea."

The two men walked through the house and round to the back yard.

Everywhere children were sorting clothes, cleaning pots and chopping wood.

"We have over a hundred children here at Hope Place," muttered Thomas Barnardo as if he was talking to himself.

"Some are old enough to work for other people and make money for the home."

"But who could organise them?" asked George Williams. "We haven't a free

moment between us."

Thomas Barnardo smiled.

"I know two boys who could help."

"You mean Toby Cutler and Jack Riley?"

"Exactly," replied Thomas Barnardo.

★ ★ ★

Five minutes later Toby Cutler and Jack Riley stood in front of Thomas Barnardo's desk.

"Nothing's wrong is there, sir," muttered Jack. Both he and Toby were so frightened, their knees were knocking. They had been at Hope Place for just over a month now and their lives had changed completely.

For the first time ever, they had breakfast in the morning and supper at night. They had a bed to sleep on and once a week there was reading and

writing. On Sundays, Dr. Barnardo even
read to them from the Bible.

Of course, there was hard work too, but
Toby and Jack were good at hard work.

Toby bit his lip. "You ain't gonna throw
us out, are you, sir?"

"Throw you out? I never throw anyone
out," replied Thomas Barnardo with a
smile. "Especially not two of the cleverest
boys in Hope Place."

He leaned back on his chair and looked very serious. "I need your help. We have to find a way of making money for the home."

Toby felt as if he was ten feet tall. He would never forget that he owed all his new-found happiness to this kind and extraordinary man.

"I want to start a business selling chopped wood, Toby," said Thomas Barnardo. "And I believe you could be be useful to me."

Toby went bright pink.

"I'll do anything I can, sir," he almost whispered.

"Excellent."

Thomas Barnardo pressed his fingers together and turned to Jack.

"You know London like the back of your hand, don't you Jack?"

"Yes sir."

"Will you help me start a message delivery service?"

Jack's face lit up. "I know all the short cuts," he almost shouted. "I'll show you."

"Not me," replied Thomas Barnardo, smiling. "Choose your boys."

"They've got to be good runners," said Jack gruffly. "I'll test 'em myself."

Thomas Barnardo looked at the two boys who only a month before had been as wild and skinny as a pair of alley cats.

With God's will, he would help hundreds more children just like them.

5

God Bless Dr. Barnardo's Boys!

Toby Cutler wanted to pinch himself. Was he really driving a proper pony trap with Jack sitting beside him? Or was it a dream?

Toby Cutler did pinch himself. It wasn't a dream! He then pinched Jack just for the fun of it.

"Ow!" cried Jack. "What did you do that for, Toby!"

"It's not a dream!" shouted Toby. He threw back his head and laughed. "We're really here!"

Jack pretended to look bad-tempered.

"We won't be anywhere if you don't follow my instructions," he muttered gruffly. "Turn left by that pillar box."

But inside Jack was just as excited as Toby. It was two years almost to the day

since Thomas Barnardo had asked them
to help raise money for the home. And
over those two years, the chopped wood
business and messenger service had been
a huge success.

Thomas Barnardo had bought another
home and was even trying to raise money
so that he could buy a tavern and turn it
into a meeting place.

This afternoon, as a mark of their
standing in the home, Toby and Jack had

been allowed to make a special delivery of chopped wood to a cabinet maker on the other side of London.

Jack punched his friend lightly on the arm. "Who would have thought it, eh?" he said. "Two starved runts like us driving about like toffs in our own wagon."

Toby grinned and tried to concentrate on guiding the pony down the crowded noisy street.

"There it is!" cried Jack pointing to the end of the street. Beyond a market stall, a flaky sign hung halfway up a brick house. SAM DAWKINS CABINET MAKER.

They turned the wagon under the sign and went into a yard.

A woman in a checked apron hurried out of the brick house. She had rosy cheeks and her brown hair was twisted into a bun. "Dr. Barnardo's boys?" she asked.

Toby and Jack nodded and jumped down from the cart.

"Which of you is Toby Cutler?"

"Me, ma'am," replied Toby quickly. "Is something wrong."

"Not at all, lad," replied the woman "Mr. Dawkins would like a word when you're finished."

"Must be another order," muttered Toby as he began to unstack the wood.

A sixth sense told Jack that it wasn't. It was something else.

Toby had a way with wood. Only last week Dr. Barnardo himself had mentioned it.

"Do you ever think about being an apprentice?" asked  Jack in an easy voice. "You know, like you thought you was going to be once."

Toby's eyes lit up. "All the time," he replied. "Then I could send my ma a sixpence like I promised. He shrugged. "But anyone can dream."

At that moment, a thick set man with

grizzled grey hair walked briskly into the yard. He wore a long leather apron with tools tucked into the leather pockets.

"Sam Dawkins," he said in a deep voice. He held out his hand to both boys.

Then he looked Toby firmly in the eye.

"I need an apprentice, Toby," said Sam Dawkins. "Dr. Barnardo says you're the lad for the job." He looked Toby straight in the eye. "Will you work for me?"

Toby was too stunned to speak.

"Yes," muttered Jack kicking him in the shins.

"Yes," cried Toby. "Yes, please!"

Sam Dawkins smiled.

"You start tomorrow."

★ ★ ★

Thomas Barnardo leaned back on his office chair. Beside him, his assistant George Williams watched as a young girl poured out four cups of tea.

"We shall celebrate with tea, Mr. Williams," said Dr. Barnardo with a smile. He motioned with his hand for Jack Riley and Toby Cutler to sit down.

Jack picked up his tea cup and almost spilt it. He was still trying hard to feel happy for Toby. But it wasn't working. The truth was he would miss his friend dreadfully.

"Cheer up, Jack," said Dr. Barnardo. "I've got a surprise for you, too." He picked up a letter. "The post office want you to work for them. You can lodge at Sam Dawkins'."

Jack's world turned upside down. So did his cup of tea. He watched

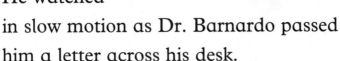

in slow motion as Dr. Barnardo passed him a letter across his desk.

"Well?"

Jack was too stunned to speak.

"Yes," muttered Toby kicking Jack in the shins.

"Yes," shouted Jack. "Yes! Yes! Thank you sir!"

"Don't thank me," replied Dr. Barnardo. "You have both been a great credit to me. Your hard work has brought its own rewards."

Thomas Barnardo lifted his cup.

"Mr. Williams," he cried. "These fine fellows are the starving urchins we found in a stable! Do you recognize them, sir?"

Jack and Toby looked at each other and grinned. They did indeed look completely different but they knew they would never forget that first night on the river.

Toby swallowed and spoke in the deepest voice he could manage.

"It is all your doing, sir," he said. "God bless you, sir."

"Well said," cried George Williams. He raised his cup first to Dr. Barnardo and then to Jack and Toby.

"God bless Dr. Barnardo's Boys!"

Notes

Dr. Barnardo

Thomas Barnardo set up the first refuge for homeless boys in 1867. It was called the East End Juvenille Mission. The boys worked at chopping wood, brushmaking, bootmaking and delivering messages to raise money for their keep. Dr. Barnardo went on to open many more homes and helped thousands of orphaned and homeless children.

London's East End

Only poor people lived in the East End of London in Victorian times. It was an overcrowded slum area. Diseases like cholera and typhoid spread easily because there was no clean water and no sewage system. More than half the children died before they were five years old.

Hard Times

In the 1850s 'stink' industries like glue and rubber factories moved into the East End. Conditions were terrible and dangerous and many men were killed. Women often did 'piece work' at home, sewing parts of garments.

Street Life

Street lighting came from gas lamps. A lamplighter went around each evening lighting the street lamps and turning them off in the morning. The East End was badly lit and bands of thieves roamed the streets picking pockets and stealing what they could to eat.

Foodsellers

Many people tried to make a living by selling food on the street. Hot potatoes cost less than a penny and were popular since poor people did not have an oven at home.

Sparks: Historical Adventures

ANCIENT GREECE
The Great Horse of Troy – The Trojan War
0 7496 3369 7 (hbk)   0 7496 3538 X (pbk)
The Winner's Wreath – Ancient Greek Olympics
0 7496 3368 9 (hbk)   0 7496 3555 X (pbk)

INVADERS AND SETTLERS
Boudicca Strikes Back – The Romans in Britain
0 7496 3366 2 (hbk)   0 7496 3546 0 (pbk)
Viking Raiders – A Norse Attack
0 7496 3089 2 (hbk)   0 7496 3457 X (pbk)
Erik's New Home – A Viking Town
0 7496 3367 0 (hbk)   0 7496 3552 5 (pbk)
TALES OF THE ROWDY ROMANS
The Great Necklace Hunt
0 7496 2221 0 (hbk)   0 7496 2628 3 (pbk)
The Lost Legionary
0 7496 2222 9 (hbk)   0 7496 2629 1 (pbk)
The Guard Dog Geese
0 7496 2331 4 (hbk)   0 7496 2630 5 (pbk)
A Runaway Donkey
0 7496 2332 2 (hbk)   0 7496 2631 3 (pbk)

TUDORS AND STUARTS
Captain Drake's Orders – The Armada
0 7496 2556 2 (hbk)   0 7496 3121 X (pbk)
London's Burning – The Great Fire of London
0 7496 2557 0 (hbk)   0 7496 3122 8 (pbk)
Mystery at the Globe – Shakespeare's Theatre
0 7496 3096 5 (hbk)   0 7496 3449 9 (pbk)
Plague! – A Tudor Epidemic
0 7496 3365 4 (hbk)   0 7496 3556 8 (pbk)
Stranger in the Glen – Rob Roy
0 7496 2586 4 (hbk)   0 7496 3123 6 (pbk)
A Dream of Danger – The Massacre of Glencoe
0 7496 2587 2 (hbk)   0 7496 3124 4 (pbk)
A Queen's Promise – Mary Queen of Scots
0 7496 2589 9 (hbk)   0 7496 3125 2 (pbk)
Over the Sea to Skye – Bonnie Prince Charlie
0 7496 2588 0 (hbk)   0 7496 3126 0 (pbk)
TALES OF A TUDOR TEARAWAY
A Pig Called Henry
0 7496 2204 4 (hbk)   0 7496 2625 9 (pbk)
A Horse Called Deathblow
0 7496 2205 9 (hbk)   0 7496 2624 0 (pbk)
Dancing for Captain Drake
0 7496 2234 2 (hbk)   0 7496 2626 7 (pbk)
Birthdays are a Serious Business
0 7496 2235 0 (hbk)   0 7496 2627 5 (pbk)

VICTORIAN ERA
The Runaway Slave – The British Slave Trade
0 7496 3093 0 (hbk)   0 7496 3456 1 (pbk)
The Sewer Sleuth – Victorian Cholera
0 7496 2590 2 (hbk)   0 7496 3128 7 (pbk)
Convict! – Criminals Sent to Australia
0 7496 2591 0 (hbk)   0 7496 3129 5 (pbk)
An Indian Adventure – Victorian India
0 7496 3090 6 (hbk)   0 7496 3451 0 (pbk)
Farewell to Ireland – Emigration to America
0 7496 3094 9 (hbk)   0 7496 3448 0 (pbk)

The Great Hunger – Famine in Ireland
0 7496 3095 7 (hbk)   0 7496 3447 2 (pbk)
Fire Down the Pit – A Welsh Mining Disaster
0 7496 3091 4 (hbk)   0 7496 3450 2 (pbk)
Tunnel Rescue – The Great Western Railway
0 7496 3353 0 (hbk)   0 7496 3537 1 (pbk)
Kidnap on the Canal – Victorian Waterways
0 7496 3352 2 (hbk)   0 7496 3540 1 (pbk)
Dr. Barnardo's Boys – Victorian Charity
0 7496 3358 1 (hbk)   0 7496 3541 X (pbk)
The Iron Ship – Brunel's Great Britain
0 7496 3355 7 (hbk)   0 7496 3543 6 (pbk)
Bodies for Sale – Victorian Tomb-Robbers
0 7496 3364 6 (hbk)   0 7496 3539 8 (pbk)
Penny Post Boy – The Victorian Postal Service
0 7496 3362 X (hbk)   0 7496 3544 4 (pbk)
The Canal Diggers – The Manchester Ship Canal
0 7496 3356 5 (hbk)   0 7496 3545 2 (pbk)
The Tay Bridge Tragedy – A Victorian Disaster
0 7496 3354 9 (hbk)   0 7496 3547 9 (pbk)
Stop, Thief! – The Victorian Police
0 7496 3359 X (hbk)   0 7496 3548 7 (pbk)
A School – for Girls! – Victorian Schools
0 7496 3360 3 (hbk)   0 7496 3549 5 (pbk)
Chimney Charlie – Victorian Chimney Sweeps
0 7496 3351 4 (hbk)   0 7496 3551 7 (pbk)
Down the Drain – Victorian Sewers
0 7496 3357 3 (hbk)   0 7496 3550 9 (pbk)
The Ideal Home – A Victorian New Town
0 7496 3361 1 (hbk)   0 7496 3553 3 (pbk)
Stage Struck – Victorian Music Hall
0 7496 3363 8 (hbk)   0 7496 3554 1 (pbk)
TRAVELS OF A YOUNG VICTORIAN
The Golden Key
0 7496 2360 8 (hbk)   0 7496 2632 1 (pbk)
Poppy's Big Push
0 7496 2361 6 (hbk)   0 7496 2633 X (pbk)
Poppy's Secret
0 7496 2374 8 (hbk)   0 7496 2634 8 (pbk)
The Lost Treasure
0 7496 2375 6 (hbk)   0 7496 2635 6 (pbk)

20th-CENTURY HISTORY
Fight for the Vote – The Suffragettes
0 7496 3092 2 (hbk)   0 7496 3452 9 (pbk)
The Road to London – The Jarrow March
0 7496 2609 7 (hbk)   0 7496 3132 5 (pbk)
The Sandbag Secret – The Blitz
0 7496 2608 9 (hbk)   0 7496 3133 3 (pbk)
Sid's War – Evacuation
0 7496 3209 7 (hbk)   0 7496 3445 6 (pbk)
D-Day! – Wartime Adventure
0 7496 3208 9 (hbk)   0 7496 3446 4 (pbk)
The Prisoner – A Prisoner of War
0 7496 3212 7 (hbk)   0 7496 3455 3 (pbk)
Escape from Germany – Wartime Refugees
0 7496 3211 9 (hbk)   0 7496 3454 5 (pbk)
Flying Bombs – Wartime Bomb Disposal
0 7496 3210 0 (hbk)   0 7496 3453 7 (pbk)
12,000 Miles From Home – Sent to Australia
0 7496 3370 0 (hbk)   0 7496 3542 8 (pbk)

Dr. Barnardo's Boys

by
Karen Wallace
Illustrations by Martin Remphry

W
FRANKLIN WATTS
NEW YORK • LONDON • SYDNEY

First published in 1999 by Franklin Watts
96 Leonard Street, London EC2A 4XD

Franklin Watts Australia
56 O'Riordan Street, Alexandria, Sydney, NSW 2015

This edition published 2002
Text © Karen Wallace 1999

Editor: Claire Berridge
Designer: Jason Anscomb
Consultant: Dr Anne Millard, BA Hons, Dip Ed, PhD

A CIP catalogue record for this book
is available from the British Library.

ISBN 0 7496 4597 0 (pbk)

Dewey Classification 362.7/941.081

Printed in Great Britain

WALLACE, K.

Dr. Barnardo's boys

Please return or renew this item by the last date shown.
You may renew items (unless they have been requested
by another customer) by telephoning, writing to or calling
in at any library.   100% recycled paper   *BKS 1 (5/95)*

Then I feel bad for thinking that. Polly can be OK sometimes. She just likes to drink, that's all.

"Listen, you're better off without him," I tell her. "He was a loser."

I try to pat her arm, but she jerks away. "Leave me alone!" she shouts. "Get out, just get out!"

Fine, if that's what she wants. I grab my things and go into my room. My heart's thumping like I've just run a race.

I sit down on my bed and take my guitar out. It makes me feel better just to look at it. I got it at a second-hand shop. It cost me a tenner. It sounds OK, even if the D string keeps slipping.

I start to play, softly so that Polly won't hear. I've never had any lessons, I just taught myself. At first I made loads of mistakes. Now I've been playing for a few years, and I'm not bad.

First I play that Robbie Williams song, 'Angel'. Then I start to play a song that I wrote myself. It's not finished yet, but I like it.

Suddenly my bedroom door bangs open, and I jump. Polly's standing there. She's got the bottle of vodka in her hand. It's empty now. Before I can do anything she starts swinging it around.

"It's all your fault!" she shouts. She hits the bottle on my clock and it goes flying.

I can't move. I've seen her drunk hundreds of times, but never as bad as this before. Her eyes are blank and staring, like she doesn't know who I am. Only she must do, because she's talking to me.

"Why did I ever have to have you?" she spits out. "Single mum at fifteen. God, what an idiot I was! I had to give up my life, my future – everything – "

SMASH! She slams the bottle on the wall. It shatters, and bits of glass go everywhere.

I'm scared, but I'm angry, too. My room is the one place in the flat that's not a tip, and now she's messing it up. The rest of the flat is full of old fag ends and empty beer cans. She never cleans, all she ever does is drink. What sort of mum is she?

"Stop it!" I shout at her.

She stares at me, breathing hard. She's still holding the bottle's neck. Its ends are jagged and pointy. "I'm going to put things right now, Luke," she says. "I'm going to get my life back on track."

I don't know what she means. Then she comes at me, she tries to cut my neck with the broken glass.

I shout out and push her away. She almost falls but then she's back at me again, snarling like an animal. She shoves the bottle neck at my face. I see a flash of sharp glass, and I put my arm up. The glass goes right into it, ripping at my skin.

Suddenly there's blood everywhere. It's on the bed, on the floor. How can all that blood come from me? Polly's still trying to get at my face, and I push her away as hard as I can. She falls onto the floor.

I feel sick as I look down at her. She's not moving. Jesus. Has she passed out? Or ... or is she dead?

Then Polly's eyelids flutter. She looks up at me.

"Get out before I kill you," she whispers.

I don't wait. Before she can move, I've grabbed my guitar and my school bag and run out the front door.

Chapter 2
On the Street

It's late at night, and I'm sitting in a Burger King in town. I had a burger, but that was a long time ago. I don't know what to do. I can't go home. I think of the look on Polly's face, and shiver. I'm never going back there again.

My arm hurts. Once I got away from the flat, I I looked at the cut. It's over over an inch long, and deep. I think it needs stitches, but I'm too scared to go to hospital. What if they found out that my mum hurt me like that? They'd put me into care.

And it sounds stupid, but I don't want to get Polly into trouble. I know she *should* get into trouble – she only bloody tried to kill me. I feel ill thinking that, but I still don't want to think about her being arrested and taken away.

So I didn't go to hospital. I tied my sports t-shirt around my arm, as tight as I could. Then I pulled my sweatshirt sleeve over it. My arm's stopped bleeding now, but it still hurts. Really badly.

A guy in a Burger King uniform is starting to mop up the floor. "Closing time, mate," he says to me.

I pretend not to hear him, and take a last gulp of my Coke.

"Oy, are you deaf?" The guy jabs my arm. "We're closing up now."

"Yeah, OK," I mutter.

Slowly, I pick up my things and leave. Damn. What now? It's winter, and too cold to sleep outside. I've only got my school sweatshirt on, and then a denim jacket over that. I'll freeze to death.

There's a pub across the road. The street outside is full of people smoking. The girls are all in short skirts, and the blokes are showing off for them, shouting and laughing. Drunken tossers.

Think, I tell myself. Where can I sleep? Where do homeless people go? There must be hostels or something, but I don't know where they are. I don't even have a mate to help me out. I don't have any friends at school.

There's a NatWest Bank beside the Burger King. I lean against the wall and start to play my guitar. It makes my arm hurt more, but the music calms me down, helps me think.

Suddenly there's someone standing beside me. "Not your normal gig, this, is it?" says a voice.

It's a guy with long brown hair and dirty old clothes. I've seen him before. He normally sits on the street and begs. I guess he's seen me too, playing my guitar in the town centre.

He leans back on the wall beside me. "I'm Dave," he says, and he holds out his hand.

I shake it. "I'm Luke," I tell him. He smells like he hasn't washed in a month. But maybe he can tell me what to do. "Listen, um ... I sort of need a place to stay. Do you know where I can go?" I ask.

He shakes his head. "Run away, eh?"

I give a shrug. "Something like that." I'm not about to tell him the truth.

He looks me over slowly. It's like he's making his mind up about something. Then he nods. "Yeah, I know where you can stay. Come on."

****

He takes me to an empty office block on the edge of town. There's graffiti all over it and the doors are all planked up. There's a fence too, but Dave shows me where you can crawl under it. I pull my guitar after me.

There are some steps going down from the road on one side. Then there's a metal door with the window broken out. "In here," says Dave. He climbs through.

Suddenly I'm not too sure about this. It's dark in there, and I don't even know this guy. What if he's a murderer? Someone's already tried to kill me once today.

But I've got nowhere else to go. So I hand my things to Dave, and then I climb in. The pain in my arm almost makes me pass out. I grit my teeth.

"You all right?" says Dave.

I nod.

"Come on." He leads the way. It's so dark I can't see much. I hear a scurrying sound – there must be rats in here. Great.

Dave pushes open a door, and suddenly there's light. We're in a hall-way, and there are light bulbs hanging down from the ceiling. They're on low and they make a buzzing sound.

I blink. "How – " I start to ask.

Dave winks. "Just like home, eh? We've even got water in the toilets."

"Why doesn't the council turn off the power?" I ask. We're walking along a corridor.

Dave opens another door and I can see a dark stair-well.

"In here," he says and starts to climb up the stairs. I go after him. "The only lights that go on are the ones they can't see outside. Got it?" he asks. "Or else Big John will have something to say to you."

He hasn't told me why the council left the power on. I don't ask him again. It doesn't take many brains to work out that the people who live here are stealing the electricity, somehow.

"Who's Big John?" I ask.

"Don't worry, you'll get to meet him," says Dave. He looks back at me with a grin. "Yeah, I reckon Big John will be very interested in you."

I don't like the sound of this. I start to tell him that I don't want any hassle, and then he pushes open another door.

Suddenly we're in a big room, with bin bags tacked up over the windows. There are about six people in there, cooking over a camp stove. I smell bacon, and my stomach growls.

Dave takes me over to meet them. There's a guy called Tom, and one called Baz, and a few others. Baz gives me some bacon, and I gulp it down. "You got any gear?" he asks me.

He means drugs. Hard stuff, like heroin. Looking around, I can see old needles on the floor. Suddenly the bacon doesn't taste very good anymore.

I shake my head. "No. Sorry."

Baz gives a sigh. "Oh, well." He lies down on the floor. Tom's sitting by himself, sort of swaying and smiling. He looks like he's already high on something. Then Dave lights up a spliff. He takes a deep drag and offers it to me.

I shake my head again. Dave frowns, and then gives a shrug. "You're into clean living, is that it? Fine, more for us." He passes the spliff to Baz.

Slowly, I eat my last bit of bacon. Clean living? God, he should see what our flat looks like! I've just never wanted to do drugs, that's all. Drink's bad enough with what it does to you. Look at Polly.

The thought of her makes me feel ... I don't know what. Sad and angry and scared, all at the same time. What's she doing now? Is she sorry she attacked me? Or is she glad I'm gone?

I'm glad I'm gone, I tell myself. Even if I'm in a dump like this. I'm never going home again. Not ever.

There's silence for a few minutes. Everyone's lost in their own thoughts. Then Baz points at my guitar case. "Hey, you got a guitar in there?"

"'Yeah," I say.

"You play? We could use a few tunes," Baz goes on.

"Yeah, he's not bad," puts in Dave. He sounds like he's choking, and then he lets out a stream of sweet-smelling smoke.

"Go on, kid, give us a tune," says someone else.

I start to open the case, and then stop. My arm is hurting, worse than before. And somehow I don't want to get out my guitar in front of them. It's the only thing I have that's truly mine.

"Nah. Maybe later," I say.

I feel the mood change. They all look really annoyed. Even Tom stops swaying and stares at me.

I try not to show how nervous I am. "Sorry. I'm just tired," I say. "Is, um – is there someplace I could bunk down?"

For a second I think Dave is going to say no. Then he sneers at me and stands up. "Yeah, come on."

"Thanks for the bacon," I say to Baz as we leave the room. He doesn't reply.

Dave takes me to a room that looks like it was an office. Now there's dirt all over the walls, and a big burnt place on the carpet, as if someone tried to set the place on fire.

Dave doesn't say anything. He just sort of points to the floor and walks off. There's no door to close, which makes me even more nervous. At least there's an old sleeping bag in one corner. It looks really dirty, but it'll do me.

It's cold in here. I keep my clothes on and get into the sleeping bag. It stinks of piss. I try not to think about it and close my eyes. I keep my guitar close beside me, where I can touch it and know it's safe.

At first I can't sleep. All I can think of is Polly, coming at me with the broken bottle. She's my mum, how could she do that to me? Does she really hate me that much?

All at once my eyes feel hot with tears. *Stop it!* I tell myself. I wipe my sleeve over my face and push the thoughts away. Forget her. She's not worth it.

Someone's laughing in the other room. I wonder if they're talking about me. I should have played my guitar for them. I was stupid – I need to stay here. *I'll do it tomorrow*, I tell myself. I'll give them a whole concert if they like.

Just as I drift off to sleep, I remember that I haven't met Big John yet.

Chapter 3
Big John

I wake up early the next morning. At first I can't think where I am, and then it all comes back. The office block is totally silent. I crawl out from the sleeping bag, and go to find the toilets.

They're dirty and they smell bad, but Dave's right – there's water in the taps. I splash some on my face and wish I could take a shower. My face in the mirror looks the same as always. How can I look so normal, after all that's happened?

I want to skip school, but I'm scared to. They'll ring Polly, and then they'll know something's wrong.

So what? I think. Let them arrest her, she deserves it!

But I just can't let that happen. So I go back into the room, get my things, and sneak out of the building. The big room has a few people sleeping in a corner. I don't see Dave anywhere, and I'm glad.

At school that day I act like everything's the same as always. I haven't done any homework, but then what's different about that? No one looks at me funny or anything, so I guess I get away with it.

When the last bell rings, I go to Mr King's room for my guitar. He's at his desk, marking papers. He's OK, for a teacher. He teaches English, but you can talk to him about other stuff too. And he's always been really interested in my music.

"All right, Luke?" he asks when he sees me.

I nod, and go and get my guitar out of his cupboard.

He grins. "When's your first concert, then, so I can come?"

I don't feel like it but this makes me smile. "Not yet, sir," I say as I pick up my guitar and leave.

Slowly I walk away from school. Could I have told Mr King what's happened to me? That Polly attacked me and threw me out. That my arm still really hurts, and I'm not sure what to do about it needing stitches.

How scared I am.

Don't be so stupid, I tell myself. Mr King seems OK, but he's still a teacher. He'd put me into care, just like anyone else.

I play for hours in the town centre that day. I play every song I know, and I sing, too. I'm losing myself in the music and enjoying it. People are stopping and listening to me. Some of them even put money on my jacket on the pavement beside me.

Suddenly I see that I've made over ten pounds. That's the most I've ever got. I stare down at the money. All at once my dream of being a rock star doesn't seem so stupid after all. With a grin, I scoop the money up and go to Burger King. I'm starving.

The happiness doesn't last very long. Neither does my burger and fries. After I eat, I just sit there and think. I don't know what to do next. I sort of thought Polly might send me a text once she was sober again, saying, *Sorry, Luke*, the next text'd say. *I didn't mean it. Please come home.*

But she hasn't.

Maybe I should go home anyway. Maybe Polly's hurt herself or something. Then I remember her face, and the way she snarled at me. It was horrible. I can't go back, not ever.

"Hi, Luke," says a voice. I look up, and it's Gemma, from school. She sits down at my table.

"I heard you playing your guitar," she says. Her blue eyes are shining. "Luke, you're really good! You should be on TV."

"Yeah?" I say.

She nods, and offers me some of her fries. "How long have you been playing?"

"A few years," I tell her. I never know what to say to girls, but Gemma keeps asking me things, and before I know it, almost an hour has passed. I know she must need to go home soon. But she doesn't seem to want to leave.

She toys with her empty burger wrapper. "Would you play something for me?" she asks.

The question makes me feel funny – sort of warm inside. I give a shrug, like I don't care.

"Now?" she asks with a smile.

"OK," I say.

We go outside and sit on a bench, and I get my guitar out. I'm not sure why, but I start playing her the song I made up, the one that doesn't have words yet. Only now the words begin to come. I sing them as I play:

I was looking all this time
Never knew it, but I was.
You made me feel so fine,
But that was yesterday.

Today it all seems changed,
So much harder than before.
I'm still looking, all the time,
I just can't find it.

25

That's all the words I've thought of so far, so I just play the music a few more times, and then finish. Gemma claps like she really means it. "Luke, what was that? It was great!"

I try not to grin like a jerk. "Just something I wrote," I say.

****

That night I go back to the office block. I don't want to, but I don't know where else to go. I have to sleep somewhere.

The building is so silent that it's creepy. I crawl under the fence. A few minutes later I'm making my way through the dark inside. Maybe I can sleep here, on the ground floor. If I can find a place here and not go upstairs, the others won't even know.

It seems like a really good idea. There's only one problem with it. When I get to the hall-way, someone's standing there waiting for me.

I know right away it's Big John. He's massive, over six feet tall, and built like a boxer. He has wild, dark hair and a big old black jacket. He smells as bad as Dave does.

"Why, hello," he says. "You must be Luke."

He's smiling, but I don't like the look in his eyes. I take a step back, and he grabs my arm.

"Lukey, Lukey, don't go yet!" He puts his arm round me like I'm his best mate. "We want you to come join the party, play some music for us. That's only fair, isn't it? Since you're staying here?"

"Um … yeah," I say.

"I think you don't trust us," he says sadly. He starts walking me towards the stairs. "You took your guitar with you today. You didn't have to do that, Luke. None of us are *thieves* here."

No, just druggies, I want to say. I swallow hard. "I trust you. I only took it with me so I could play in town today. Make some dosh, you know?"

Then I wish I hadn't said that. Big John stops walking and looks at me. "Oh? Did you make much?"

I shake my head. "Nah, just a few quid. I spent it all on food." I don't tell him that I've still got five pounds left. I may need it.

Big John makes a *tutting* noise. "Now, Lukey, that's not how it works here. This place isn't free, you know. We all have to share." He gives me a prod. "We're all one big, happy family!"

Suddenly I'm really scared. I want to run for it, but he's still got his arm round me. And I have a feeling that he's a lot faster than he looks. If I tried to do a runner, he'd get me.

He takes me upstairs to the big room. Dave and Baz are there, and Tom. They're all passing around a bottle of whisky. I don't want to stay, but Big John sits on the floor and pulls me down beside him.

"Hey, Luke, how's it going?" says Dave. "Here, warm yourself up." He holds out the bottle.

"Uh – no, thanks," I say.

Big John takes the bottle and shoves it into my hand. "You're not very polite, are you,

Luke?" he says. "We're having a party here. Now, drink up and get happy with us."

No one says anything. They're all looking at me, waiting to see what I'll do. Big John's eyes are as hard as steel, and I know I don't have a choice.

So I lift the bottle to my lips and I take a drink.

Chapter 4

The Party

I'm flying. I'm on top of the world.

The whisky bottle is almost empty now. I take another swig when it's passed to me, and then another. It burns my throat, but it tastes great. It wakes you up, makes you feel alive. *So this is why Polly likes getting drunk so much*, I think. I don't blame her.

Big John laughs and pulls the bottle away from me. "Oy, save some for the rest of us."

"Another song!" calls out Dave and he slaps the floor with his hand.

I've been playing for hours already, but I don't care. I want to play on and on, and never stop.

I play an old song by The Beatles. Everyone sings along, but I sing louder than anyone and I belt the words out like a rock star. They shout and clap.

"Go *Luke!*" says Baz.

Why didn't I trust them before? They're all really good guys. They're my mates. I've never had mates before, and now I do. I fit in here, I belong. I'll never have to go home again. I'll just live here always, with my friends Big John and Dave and Baz.

I try to tell them how I feel, but I can't talk properly. "You guys are the best," I say. It sounds like my mouth's full of big stones. I stop. Why can't I talk? What's wrong with me?

Dave takes my guitar and starts to strum it. He's really rubbish. I start to tell him, but then I see that there's two Daves. Two Daves and two guitars.

Suddenly my stomach's churning, and I feel dizzy. There's two of everyone. Baz is getting a needle out and tying a cloth round his arm. I can't see him properly. He goes in and out of focus as he pulls the cloth tight with his teeth. Then Big John is there, his face large, right next to mine.

"Come on, Lukey," he says. His voice is soft and gentle. "Time for bed."

****

When I wake up, I don't know where I am. All I know is that my head is thudding, and I'm so thirsty. I'm lying on a mattress and right next to me I can hear someone snoring.

And ... there's an arm round me, hugging me tight. My heart thumps as I stare at it. It's big, and hairy.

What the hell?

I shove the arm off me and get up. *Where are my trousers?* I see them in the middle of the floor, near the burnt patch. And it's Big John who's lying on the mattress.

His eyes open, and he sits up. He's only wearing his trousers and the flies are undone. His fat, hairy belly hangs over the top of them.

"Morning, Luke," he says. Just like everything's normal.

"What's going on?" I say. I grab my trousers and pull them on. My voice is high and scared. "What – did you do? What's going on?"

His teeth are yellow as he grins. "What would you like me to do?"

I think I'm going to be sick. Then I see that my guitar's gone. I start to run for the door, but suddenly Big John's blocking my way. "My guitar!" I shout at him. "Where is it? Is it in the other room?"

He looks smug. Suddenly I know that I won't find my guitar, no matter how much I look. He's taken it.

"Luke, come on," he says. "A deal's a deal. You know that you gave me your guitar last night, to help pay for staying here."

"You're lying," I tell him. I might have been drunk, but I know I'd never say that. I'd die before I gave away my guitar.

Big John goes silent, staring at me. "I'm what?" he says.

"You're lying!" I yell. I feel like crying. "Where's my guitar, you thief – "

He hits me across the side of my head, and I cry out. It's like stars are rushing past me.

"Now listen," he hisses and he puts his face right up close to mine. "I've been very nice to you so far. I didn't even touch you last night. But you've stayed at Hotel Big John for two days now, Lukey-boy, and it's time to pay up. You'll get your guitar back when I say so."

"What – what do you want?" I stammer. But I think I already know.

"Nothing much," he says. He touches my face with a finger. "Just for you to be nice to me, that's all. And then maybe you can be nice to a few other people, too. Wouldn't you like that?"

I can't move. I can't say anything. I'd throw up if I tried to.

He strokes my cheek. "A good-looking boy like you ... you'd make a lot more money being nice, you know, than you ever would playing your guitar – "

All at once I come to life. My knee comes up, and I knee him in the balls as hard as I can. He shouts out in pain, bends over, and I run, faster than I've ever run before. I run out of the door of the main room, and pound down the stairs, and then, at last – I'm out into the sunshine of the cold winter's day.

****

I don't know why I go to school. I guess it's just that I don't have anywhere else to go. I sit at the back all day and don't say anything. When I go to the toilet, I see a mark on my face where Big John hit me.

It hurts.

I can't believe he took my guitar. He took my mobile and my wallet, too – they're not in my pocket any more. And I forgot my school bag when I ran off. All I have left are my keys. Not that they'll do me much good now.

During RE, Gemma turns round and smiles at me. I ignore her. She looks hurt, but I don't care. It's better for her not to be friends with me.

I feel sick every time I think of Big John. He says he didn't do anything to me last night, but what if he was lying?

My head hurts. My arm hurts. I wish I was dead.

When the last bell rings, I start to walk slowly out of school. I don't want to be there, but I don't want to leave, either. What am I going to do? I don't have my guitar any more, so I can't get money by playing on the street. And what if Dave or Big John or one of the others sees me?

"Luke!" calls a voice. I turn around, and it's Mr King.

"I didn't see you this morning," he says and walks up to me. "Didn't you bring your guitar today?"

"No," I say. I try to sound like I don't care, so he'll leave me alone. But he's staring at my face. I know he sees the mark where Big John hit me.

"Luke ... is everything OK?" he asks. He seems worried.

"Fine," I mutter. I try to walk away, but he stops me.

"Listen," he says. "If something's wrong, it's OK to ask for help. You know that, don't you? Everyone needs help sometimes, it's no big deal."

He puts his hand on my arm. Teachers shouldn't do that. They shouldn't touch you. I pull away from him.

"Bog off!" I snarl.

He looks shocked. "Luke, I was only trying to – " he starts to say.

Who cares? I walk away while he's still talking.

****

I go to a part of town where I've never been before. It's full of trees and big houses. All the little old ladies glare at me, like they wish I wasn't there.

I'm starving. I haven't eaten since yesterday. I feel like a jerk, but I stand in front of a posh-looking pub and begin to sing.

It's awful. People look embarrassed when they see me. No one gives me any money. I feel so stupid, but I keep singing. I don't know what else to do.

Suddenly a man comes out of the pub. He's wearing an apron, and he looks really cross.

"What do you think you're doing?" he snaps. "Get out of here, before I call the cops."

Tosser. Does he think I'm doing this for fun?

He takes a step forward. "Go on, I said leave!"

My face feels on fire as I walk away. I walk for a long time. In the end, I come to a park, and I sit down on one of the benches. I'm so tired. Why didn't I tell that man from the pub to go ahead and call the cops? At least then I'd have somewhere to stay tonight. A police cell'd be a lot better than the streets.

I lean my head back and shut my eyes. I remember what Mr King told me – that it's OK to ask for help. That's easy for him to say. He doesn't have a clue what my life is like.

I think about Polly. What's she doing now? I've been gone for over two days. Does she even know?

It hurts to think of her. I know she's a drunk, but she can be nice sometimes, too. Sometimes we'd have a real laugh, watching TV together. Then other times she'd get angry and swear at me, because she had me too young and never got to be a teenager. But that wasn't my fault. I never asked to be born.

You should love your mum, but I don't know if I do. Sometimes I even think I hate her. But I still don't want anyone to hurt her. I know how she'd look if I turned her in. It makes me feel bad even thinking about it.

I stand up. Forget all this thinking. It's doing my head in. And I can't stay here in the park – Dave or anyone could see me.

I start walking again. It's dark now, and I'm cold. I blow on my hands to try and warm them. Where the hell am I going to sleep?

Then I see it. There's a car parked by the side of the road. A posh shiny one, with leather seats.

And it's not locked.

Chapter 5

Polly

I open the car door. I expect an alarm to go off, but nothing happens. The street is dark and silent around me.

The car's really clean inside, and smells of new leather. I get into the driver's seat and run my hands over the steering wheel. God, what would it be like to own a car like this?

I'll have lots of cars when I'm a rock star, I tell myself. One for every day of the week.

Then I drop my hands from the steering wheel. Yeah, right. Who am I kidding? I'll never be a rock star. I don't even have a guitar now.

I shove the thought away and crawl into the back seat. It's really soft, even softer than my bed at home. I don't think I'll be able to sleep, but I'm so tired that I drop off in just a few minutes.

The next thing I know, someone's banging on the car window. I wake up with a jump. It's morning, and there's a man in a suit standing there.

"What the hell are you doing in my car?" he shouts.

He swings open the door. Quickly, I open the door on the other side and get out. I hit my arm on the side of the car. It's the same arm that Polly stabbed, and it really hurts. But I don't slow down, and I run as fast as I can down the street.

The man doesn't chase me. I guess he's just happy to have his car back. When I'm a few streets away, I stop and rest my hands on my knees. I'm panting so hard I can barely breathe.

An old woman stops beside me. "Are you all right?" she asks.

I can't really talk yet, so I just nod. What can I say? *Yes, thanks – the guy whose car I slept in didn't catch me, plus I didn't freeze to death last night, so life's great!*

She looks at me. "Here," she says – and she gives me a pound coin. I can hardly believe it. I stare at her as she walks away.

There's a shop nearby, so I go in and buy a Coke and a Snickers bar. I gulp them down in about two seconds flat.

It's the last food that I have all day.

****

I know I can't go back to school, not with Mr King wanting to know what's going on with me. So I just walk. The streets change from posh to run-down, and then to something in-between. It gets dark again, and I sleep in a shop door. I shiver all night and don't sleep, because I'm so scared of Big John finding me.

Around dawn, I start walking again. My stomach is so empty that it hurts.

Suddenly I freeze. There's a massive man with long hair heading towards me. It looks like he's drunk – he's swaying to and fro. Big John! I duck around a corner and press myself flat against the wall.

Don't see me, please don't see me, I pray, as his foot-steps pass by. After a long time, I peer out. The man's crossing the road. It's not Big John at all – just some drunk who looks like him.

I slump back against the wall. I should feel glad, but suddenly I think, *If it had been Big John, maybe he'd have given me some money to be 'nice' to him.*

I'm too hungry to feel upset at what I've just thought. In fact, I'm so hungry that I start to think being with Big John wouldn't be so bad, if he'd just give me something to eat.

Good idea, whispers my hunger. *Why don't you go back to Big John's Hotel and see if he's there?*

I'm going mad. I have to do something. I take off my jacket and push up the sleeve of my sweatshirt.

My sports t-shirt is still tied round my arm. There's blood all over it. Slowly, I untie it. When I get down to where the cut is, the shirt sticks to my skin.

I grit my teeth and yank it off. The pain wakes me up, and makes me feel more like myself.

The cut is all red and lumpy. It's getting better, but it looks a mess – the ends of it haven't joined up properly, and part of it has opened up again, and oozes blood.

I stare down at it. Maybe I'm thick like Polly says. But I can see that there's not much a doctor could do for it now. That scar is going to look awful all my life. I don't care about the scar, but it just all seems so stupid. Why did Polly do this to me? Does she really hate me that much?

It starts to rain – big, cold drops that feel like ice. I shiver, and suddenly I know that I have to face her again. I can't spend the rest of my life running away.

So I put my jacket back on and I head for home.

It takes me a long time. I'm dizzy, and I keep getting lost. But I get there at last. I stand in front of the front door to our flat and listen. The only sound is the TV.

Now that I'm here I don't want to go in, but I know I have to. I can't live on the streets all my life.

I take a deep breath and unlock the door and go inside.

It smells awful, like stale food and sweat. The only light is from the TV. Polly's lying on the sofa with a duvet over her.

She sits up when I come in. "Who's that?" She turns on a lamp and stares at me. "Luke?" she whispers.

I don't know what to say. Suddenly it seems almost funny. *Hi, I know you tried to stab me, but I'm back now! How have you been?*

"Hi," I mutter. I feel really nervous. What is she going to do?

To my surprise, she starts to cry. "Oh, Luke!" she wails. She comes over to me and hugs me tight. "Where have you been? I've been so, so worried about you!"

It's like she's a proper mum in a TV show. I can tell that she's drunk, but I'm so glad to see her that I can't help hugging her back. On the table I can see another empty bottle. I try not to think about it.

Then Polly pulls away from me. "Why did you *do* that?" she shouts. "Why did you run off like that? Didn't you care how worried I'd be?"

I can't believe it. It's like she doesn't even remember. "But – you threw me out," I say.

It's as if I've slapped her. "Luke!" she cries, "I would *never* do that! How can you say that?"

Suddenly I'm more angry than I've ever been before. Everything I went through was because of her, and now she says I'm a bloody liar! I take off my jacket and show her the cut on my arm.

"You did that!" I snap. "Look! You were drunk, and you took a broken bottle and – "

"I did not!" she shouts. "You must have got into a fight or something. You're always doing things like that – "

I can't listen any more. I take the empty vodka bottle and I smash it against the table. It breaks into a hundred pieces. I shove the neck at her, and she screams and backs away.

All at once I start to cry. I don't even try to stop, I just hold the broken bottle in front of her. "No, it was you," I say. "Just like this. You told me that you'd kill me if I didn't get out."

We stare at each other. Her eyes fill up, and for a moment I think that she understands. Maybe she'll hug me again now, and say, *Oh, Luke, I'm so sorry. I never meant to hurt you. I need help, and I'll get it, you'll see.*

But then she rubs her eyes and stares back at me.

"You little shit," she says. "How dare you accuse me?"

She goes into her bedroom and slams the door. I can hear her open her wardrobe door. That's where she keeps her booze.

I feel frozen. She doesn't care at all about what she did to me. She's just going to keep drinking and drinking until she passes out. Or until she goes mad and comes after me again.

I feel like shouting, yelling, smashing things up. But I don't. I drop the bottle neck onto the floor. We don't have a land-line phone, but Polly's mobile is in the kitchen. It's still got some credit left.

I think about the way she'd look at me if they took her away. I think about all the times I've tried to look after her.

And then I look at my arm again, and I dial 999. I tell them exactly what Polly did to me. "Please send help," I say. My throat is dry. "My mum and I ... we both need help."

I'm not crying any more. I feel like I'll never cry again.

****

Later that night, after the police have taken my statement, they take me to a group home for teenagers.

"Here we are," says one of the PCs as he rings the bell.

I'm staring straight ahead like I don't care about anything. Not about being here, and not about Polly being arrested ... but inside I feel like a guitar string that's so tight that it's about to snap.

Then a girl with long blonde hair comes to the door.

Gemma.

I stare at her. "What – what are you doing here?" I stammer.

"Hi, Luke," she smiles. "I live here."

Afterwards
My Song

I've been at the group home for almost two months now. I don't like it, but it's a lot better than my real home. And at least Gemma's here. We've got to be really good friends.

I've never had many friends before. I was always too worried about them seeing Polly passed out on the floor or something. Gemma understands all that. Her old man was a drunk, too, before he topped himself. She was the one who found him. How bad is that?

I guess people like her do have problems, after all.

But there's one thing I haven't told Gemma. When she asked me where I went when I left home, I told her that I slept in the park. That's what I told the police, too. I can't tell anyone about Big John. Not yet. Maybe someday I will, but right now I just want to forget all of that.

Nothing happened to me, that's the main thing. That's what I keep telling myself.

The best part about being in the group home is that Tony, one of the youth workers, gave me his old guitar. It's in return for me working hard at school, but I know that he won't take it back.

Tony's cool. He and Gemma are the only people who I've ever told about my dream of being a rock star. And they don't think it's stupid. "Go for it!" says Tony. "Why not?"

So I spend a lot of time in my room, playing the guitar. Sometimes some of the other kids come in and listen. I don't mind. If I'm going to be a rock star, I've got to play in front of a crowd sometimes.

Polly's in rehab now. She's been there for over a month. The social workers say that she's got to dry out before she can have me back. I don't know if she even *wants* me back, or if I want to go back to her, but I guess we're stuck with each other.

Tony's taken me to visit her a few times. Before, she always did all the talking, but now she doesn't say very much. In fact, it's like she's shy. It's almost like she's scared of me.

"I don't remember a lot that happened," she said softly, the last time I saw her. "But, Luke – maybe you and I can make a fresh start, all right?"

She never said anything about my arm. And she still hasn't said that she's sorry. Maybe you can't be sorry for something you don't remember.

Anyway, I guess it's a fresh start, like she said. Tony says that I've only ever known Polly drunk, and now I have to get to know her sober.

If she stays that way ...

I take my new guitar to school with me a lot, and keep it in Mr King's room just like before. I trust the other kids here at the group home – but I just like to play at lunch sometimes, or during break.

"Hey, Luke," Mr King said to me the other day. "When's your first concert, so I can come?"

"Next week, sir," I told him with a grin.

It's true. I'm playing in the school concert. I'm going to play that song I made up. Can you believe it? Gemma talked me into it. The rest of the words to the song just came to me one day, when I was messing about on the guitar.

I was looking all this time
Never knew it, but I was.
You made me feel so fine,
But that was yesterday.

Today it all seems changed,
So much harder than before.
I'm still looking, all the time,
I just can't find it.

But now I'm playing for keeps.
You know I'm playing for keeps.
'Cos it's my life, and
I'm playing for keeps

From this point on.

When I sang it to Gemma, I looked up after I'd finished and she was crying. "Hey," I said, trying to joke. "It's not that bad, is it?"

"No," said Gemma. "It's amazing."

So now I'm playing the song in the concert. I know it's a bit naff, but I'm sort of excited anyway. Maybe everyone will think it's rubbish, but maybe they won't. There's only one way to find out.

Gemma asked me the other day if I think Polly will stay sober. How should I know? If I had to make a bet, I'd bet on her going back on the drink. I don't think that she's going to change, not when she won't even look at my arm and see what she did to me.

I hope I'm wrong, but in a way it doesn't really matter. I know I'll be OK, somehow, if she stays sober or not. I'm not alone now. I've got friends that I can count on.

And even better ... I can count on myself.

Which is pretty cool, you know?

Our books are tested
for children and young people by
children and young people.

Thanks to everyone who consulted on
a manuscript for their time and effort in
helping us to make our books better
for our readers.